The Pride Stre  KU-300-798

3

You Can't Be A Kid For Ever

Mike Wilson

Published in association with
The Basic Skills Agency

Acknowledgements
Cover: Stuart Williams/The Organisation.
Illustrations: Jim Eldridge.

Orders: please contact Bookpoint Ltd, 39 Milton Park, Abingdon, Oxon OX14 4TD. Telephone: (44) 01235 400414, Fax: (44) 01235 400454. Lines are open from 9.00–6.00, Monday to Saturday, with a 24 hour message answering service. Email address: orders@bookpoint.co.uk

British Library Cataloguing in Publication Data
A catalogue record for this title is available from The British Library

ISBN 0 340 74711 0

First published 1999
Impression number   10 9 8 7 6 5 4 3 2 1
Year   2004 2003 2002 2001 2000 1999

Typeset by Fakenham Photosetting Ltd, Fakenham, Norfolk
Printed in Great Britain for Hodder & Stoughton Educational, a division of Hodder Headline Plc, 338 Euston Road, London NW1 3BH by Athenaeum Press, Gateshead, Tyne & Wear.

JOHN / BONE

WESLEY / TALL

LUKE / SKY

SIMON / CUSTARD

CARL / SPOT

iii

We are the Pride Street Crew.
Bone, and Tall,
and Custard, and Spot
and me.

Our real names are John,
and Wesley,
and Simon and Carl.

And I'm Luke.

The Pride Street Crew began
as a five-a-side football team.
We lost,
but that is another story.

The Pride Street Crew
didn't last long.

This is the story
of how we fell apart.

We never fell out,
or anything like that.
I still see them around.
We just grew up.

You can't be a kid for ever,
can you?
You grow up,
don't you?

You grow apart.

One day,
I saw Spot outside school.
He was with Holly,
his girlfriend.
They were walking
and talking.
Hand in hand.

Spot didn't say anything to me.
He just looked at me.
Hard.
That look said:

If you call me Spot, you're dead.

'Hello, Carl,' I said.

No more Spot.
Carl and I
were growing apart.

Tall was always
good at football.
He played in goal
for the school.

Then he got into
a local team.
After that,
we didn't see him much.
He was always training.

Then Tall had a trial
for United.

I saw him the next day.
'Hey, Tall!' I said,
'how did the trial go?'

'Don't call me that, man,'
said Tall.
'I'm not a little boy
no more.'

'Sorry,' I said.
'How did the trial go, Wesley?'

No more Tall.
Wesley and I
were growing apart.

One night,
I went to see Custard.
His Dad came to the door.

'Hello, Mr Dodds,' I said.
'Is Custard in?'

'Who?'

'Custard.'

'You mean Simon,' said Mr Dodds.

'No,' said Mr Dodds.
'Simon is not coming
out to play.
Not with you.
Not with anyone.
He has got better things to do.

'Simon is staying in
to do his homework.
You know what GCSEs are,
don't you?'

No more Custard.
Simon and I
were growing apart.

A few weeks ago,
I saw Bone in town.
I was with my Mum.
He was at the back
of the market.
He was standing
by the bins.
He was waiting.

Bone looked at me.
Then he looked away.

Just then a car pulled up.
It was a smooth black car.
Bone went over.

The black window
opened an inch.
Bone put his head in.

It only took a second.

Then Bone stood up,
and went back to the bins.
The car pulled away.
So smooth.

Where did Bone
get the money?
I don't know.
I just hope he gets over this.

And then I went
and got a job.
Well, it's not a real job.
It's just helping out
on my Uncle's market stall.

It can be hard work.
But it's good
to have a bit of money
to spend!

Now I work some evenings,
and I work all day
Saturday.

I don't see the Crew
any more.

But I did see Bone
one more time.

I was working
on the market.
I was taking the rubbish
out to the bins.

Bone was out there.
He was with two older boys.
He was a mess.

'Can you lend us some money?'
he asked.

I asked him,
'What do you want money for?'

He said he was going
to London.
Things were better
in London, he said.

'I got no money,' I said.
It was the truth.
'My Uncle hasn't paid me
yet this week.'

'There's money
on the market stall,
isn't there?'
said Bone.
'Get me some of that.
I need it bad, Luke!'

I backed away.

'You need help, John,' I said.
'You need to sort yourself out.
Don't ask me
to steal for you!'

Bone looked hurt.
'Are you my friend, or what?'

'No,' I said.
'I'm not your friend.
You won't have any friends
if you don't sort yourself out!'

He called me some names, then.

I went back into the market
and told my Uncle
all about it.
That was the last
I ever saw
of John Bell.

No more Bone.
Bone and I
had grown apart.

I still see the others
from time to time.

I can see Wesley
any time I like –
playing in goal
for United's youth team.

For a time,
Carl was always in town
with his new girlfriend, Lizzy.
(Holly didn't last long.)

But then Carl's Dad
got a new job.
Carl had
to move away.

And I saw Simon Dodds.
He was coming out
of a bookshop in town.
Arms full of books ...

I was going to shout 'Custard!'
Just to see
what he would do.

But then I said to myself: No.
He isn't Custard any more.
He isn't a kid any more.

You can't be a kid for ever.
Can you?